This book belongs to:

_____

THE OLD MAN AND THE FLEA

BY **MARY ELIZABETH HANSON**
ILLUSTRATED BY **DAVID WEBBER MERRELL**

rising moon

The illustrations were rendered in watercolor and pastel
The text type was set in Giovanni Book and Giovanni Book Italic
The display type was set in Circus Mouse-Cutout
Composed in the United States of America
Designed by Lois A. Rainwater
Edited by Aimee Jackson
Production supervised by Lisa Brownfield

Printed in Hong Kong by Midas Printing Limited

www.northlandpub.com

FIRST IMPRESSION
ISBN 0-87358-776-6

Library of Congress Catalog Card Number 00-048187
Hanson, Mary Elizabeth.
The old man and the flea / Mary Elizabeth Hanson ; illustrated by David Webber Merrell.
p.   cm.
Summary: An old man and his pet flea have wonderful times together
until the townspeople think he is talking to himself.
ISBN 0-87358-776-6 (alk. paper)
[1. Fleas—Fiction. 2. Pets—Fiction.] I. Merrell, David Webber, date. ill. II. Title.

PZ7.H1988 O1 2001

[E]—dc21   00-048187

107/7.5M/2-01

To my parents, Stephen and Lois Nemcik,
for the love, laughter, and lima beans.

— M. E. H.

To my parents, Louis W. Merrell and Judy A. Merrell,
for always encouraging my love of art.

— D. W. M.

THE OLD MAN HAD LIVED ALONE

for so long, nobody would have ever believed

that one day he might go shopping for a pet.

But that's just what he did.

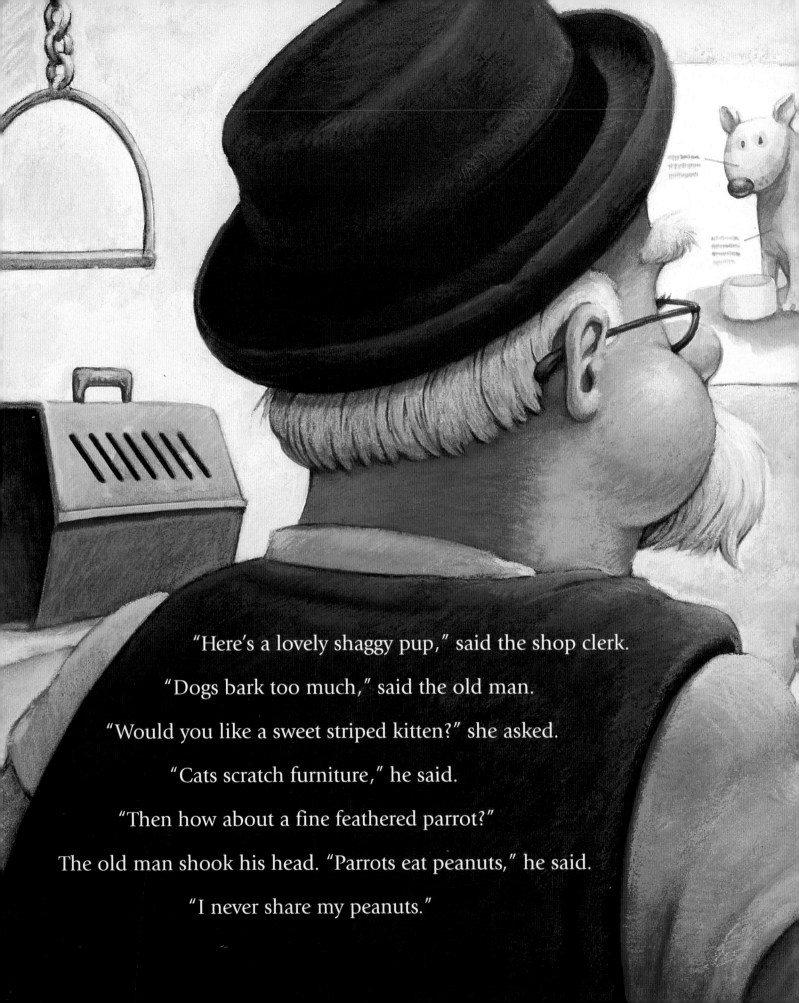

"Here's a lovely shaggy pup," said the shop clerk.

"Dogs bark too much," said the old man.

"Would you like a sweet striped kitten?" she asked.

"Cats scratch furniture," he said.

"Then how about a fine feathered parrot?"

The old man shook his head. "Parrots eat peanuts," he said.

"I never share my peanuts."

"That's all we have, sir, unless—" said the clerk, "you would like a flea."

"But fleas live on furry animals and bite people," said the old man.

"Oh no, sir," promised the lady. "This is a special breed of flea. She sleeps in a matchbox, hates fur, and never bites people." And the clerk opened a silk-lined matchbox to show off the pedigreed flea.

"She's beautiful!" said the old man. "But is she house-trained?"

"Of course, sir," said the lady. "All she needs is this teeny tiny litter tray and you're all set!"

"Splendid!" said the old man. He paid for the flea, the matchbox, and the tray and carried them all home in a little brown bag.

The old man loved the flea.

There were joys in having a pet flea
the shop clerk didn't mention.

They had hours of fun
playing leapfrog.

At the movie theater,
the old man didn't have
to buy an extra ticket.

On hot days
at the beach,
they shared a towel.

And, when they
ate in restaurants,
the flea ordered
very little.
She was truly
the perfect pet.

And life would have been perfect but for one little problem.

The townspeople began to notice that the old man seemed to be talking to himself.

"What's happened to the old man?" someone would ask.

"He's knotted his noodle."

"His toupee's too tight."

"There's a chipmunk in his chimney."

It went on like that for days.

And then one morning on a whale-watching trip,

the mayor saw the old man standing alone

and heard him talking: "Did you remember your

sunscreen? No? Then hold still." And he

carefully rubbed lotion on the flea's cheeks.

That was all the mayor needed to hear. "His cork

is cracked and the jar is empty," she thought.

She ran to the captain, who called for

an ambulance to meet the boat at the dock.

The paramedics were waiting for the old man at the end of the gangplank. He smiled, but then stopped and called to the flea, who was arguing with a pelican.

"Now, now," he said. "Let him have the popcorn. I'll make more when we get home."

"Crackers!" said the mayor to the captain.

"Pickles and tea biscuits!" said one paramedic to another.

And they wrapped him in a blanket.

"Here, here!" said the old man. "What do you think you're doing?"

"We're taking you for a nice little rest," they said, placing him in the ambulance.

"This is outrageous!" said the old man. "You must release me immediately!"

"There, there," said the mayor. "You just need someone to talk to."

And they closed the door.

"Oh, dear," said the old man as the engine started. "Whatever will become of my pet? Who will read her bedtime stories? Who will play hopscotch with her? Who will cook her spaghetti with giant meatballs?"

He worried all the way to the hospital.

At last the ambulance came to a stop, and the old man was eased into a wheelchair. He did not see the flea, who was clinging to the flashing red light on top of the ambulance.

He did not hear her bouncing behind as they wheeled him away.

He never suspected that she was hiding under the bed while the nurse tucked him in and locked the door for safekeeping.

So when the flea finally hopped up for a hug, the old man was astonished.

And when she skipped over and disappeared into the keyhole, he was positively intrigued.

He climbed out of bed, peeked into the lock, and found the flea with her back feet against the tumbler. With a delicate touch and surprising strength, she pushed and pushed until, at last, the tumbler turned. The door unlocked.

On silent, sneaky feet, the old man and the flea tiptoed through the halls. They scooted past the nurse's station. They streaked past the doctor's lounge. And soon, they were safely outside and headed for home.

By the time hospital officials discovered the empty bed, the old man and the flea had already bought another pet.

The townspeople felt much better knowing

that he had someone to talk to.

And the old man found he actually liked

sharing his peanuts.

About the Author

MARY ELIZABETH HANSON *grew up in California and can't remember a day without the companionship of at least one good pet. Over the years, her friends have been dogs, cats, birds, rats, fish and polliwogs, but no fleas. At least none that were invited to stay.*

Mary earned her Master of Library Science from UCLA, and is a former children's librarian. She has written two previous books about animals: Foghorn *(Willowisp, 1994) and* Snug *(Simon & Schuster, 1998). Mary lives in Santa Barbara, California, with her husband, two children, one dog, and three cats.*

About the Illustrator

DAVID WEBBER MERRELL *developed a love for drawing at the age of three—a hobby that has now become his full-time career. At the age of seven, he began taking art lessons from Oklahoma western artist, Fred Olds, from whom he learned cartoon and caricature techniques. David also enrolled in a basic drawing course at the University of Central Oklahoma becoming one of the school's youngest students.*

David received his degree in Graphic Design from Oklahoma State University/Okmulgee and has been a freelance illustrator ever since. His clients include Pepsi, American Airlines, Arizona Highways, *Portal Publications, Scholastic Inc., and Ziff-Davis Publishing. David currently resides in Oklahoma City, Oklahoma.*